DATE DUE

For Katie May - P.H.
To Karl, with love - D.H.

First edition for the United States
published by Barron's Educational Series, Inc., 1998.

First published in Great Britain in 1998 by
Hutchinson Children's Books
Random House UK Limited
20 Vauxhall Bridge Road
London SW1V 2SA

Text copyright © 1998 Peter Harris
Illustrations © 1998 Doffy Weir

All inquiries should be addressed to:
Barron's Educational Series, Inc.,
250 Wireless Boulevard
Hauppauge, New York 11788

Library of Congress Catalog Card No. 97-77900

ISBN 0-7641-0667-8

Printed in Singapore
9 8 7 6 5 4 3 2 1

BOTTOMLEY
at the Cattery

by Peter Harris & illustrated by Doffy Weir

BARRON'S

Me? Mope because you were away on vacation?
Of course I didn't!

I simply made the best of it,
like the sensible cat I am.

BARRETT'S
Luxury CATTERY
for
Classy Cats

BARRETT'S
Luxury CATTERY
for
Classy Cats

miaow

And I didn't fret
or fuss one little bit...

"Bottomley!" Mr. and Mrs. Barrett kept saying. "We just love having you in our cattery...

...because you're not
a scrap of trouble."

Well, you know me!

I'm not one to complain.

Some cats may expect special treatment.

...three good meals a day...

...and I'm happy.

That's what made me so popular with the other cats.

I soon became a favorite of the Barretts, too.

They couldn't do enough for me...

...and the friends I'd made kept calling in.

So with a little bit of give and take...

...the cattery became quite a home from home.

My mates were really sorry to see me go.

Bye-bye, Mr. and Mrs. Barrett.

I can't wait to come back again next year!